Bradley United Methodist Church
PENNSYLVANIA AND MAIN STREETS
GREENFIELD, INDIANA 46140

I'm Going to Run Away!

Jean Thompson

Illustrated by
Bill Myers

ABINGDON PRESS

NASHVILLE • NEW YORK

Library of Congress Cataloging in Publication Data

THOMPSON, JEAN, 1933-
I'm going to run away.

SUMMARY: One particularly bad day Jimmy de-
cides to run away but has a difficult time finding a
new home. [1. Runaways—Fiction] I. Title.
PZ7.T371595I'm   [E]   74-9760

ISBN 0-687-18676-5

To My Parents

As soon as Jimmy opened his eyes in the morning, he knew everything was going to be wrong, and he was right.

His two favorite shirts were dirty, and he had to wear one he didn't like at all. He had trouble tying his shoes. The shoelaces just wouldn't go where they should. He started over several times, but still ended up with a lopsided bow on one shoe and a floppy lace on the other.

He scuffed downstairs to the kitchen.

"Good morning, Jimmy," said his mother, and she hugged him. "What do you want for breakfast?"

"Corn flakes," he said.

His mother looked in the cupboard. "Oh, dear. We're all out. I'll fix you an egg instead."

"I don't want egg," he said, but she seemed not to hear him.

The night before, Jimmy had made a beautiful fort in the sandbox, and after he ate he went there to play with his toy soldiers. But he had forgotten to put the cover on the sandbox. Mickey, the dog next door, had been digging in it. Nothing was left of the fort but one wall.

He didn't see the dog anywhere, but he yelled, "Mickey, you're a bad, bad dog!" as loud as he could, just in case he was somewhere listening.

Jimmy then went to his best friend
Steve's house. No one answered the door.
He swung in Steve's swing, but that
wasn't much fun either.

He sat on his own porch awhile with his chin in his hands until suddenly he had a great idea. He rushed in the house, calling "Mom! Mom!"

"What is it?" She shut off the vacuum machine to listen to him.

"I know what we can do today. You can take me to Andy's house, and I can play with him."

"Andy lives twenty miles away. I'm cleaning and don't have time to go."

"Everything's awful today!" Jimmy yelled. "I'm not having any fun at all! And I'm going to run away!"

Jimmy got his bubble gum and his teddy bear and his new red jacket and put them in a shopping bag. They didn't look like very many things to take when he was running away forever, so he put in his pajamas, his toothbrush, and a book. The bag still wasn't full so he added a yellow road grader.

Bradley United Methodist Church
PENNSYLVANIA AND MAIN STREETS
GREENFIELD, INDIANA 46140

When he came into the living room, his mother was sitting on the couch. "Where are you going?" she asked.

"I'm going to find someplace else to live. Someplace where everybody will be nicer to me."

"It may be hard to find another home," she said. "Most people already have their own families."

"Somebody will want a new little boy," he said positively.

"Don't go off the street," his mother said.

Jimmy just looked at her and went out the door. When he got to the sidewalk, he turned and looked back. She was watching out the window. He thought she might call to him or wave or something, but she didn't and he went on.

He went back to Steve's house. He was sure he could live there and be Steve's brother, but Steve and his family still weren't home.

Jimmy decided to go to Mrs. Walters. She was always nice to him, and he felt she probably wouldn't mind another grandchild.

Mrs. Walters came to the door. "Good morning, Jimmy. What do you have in that big bag?"

"Everything I own," he said. "I've run away from my old home, and I'm looking for a new one. Can I live here?"

"Oh, dear! That would be a problem right now. Louise and the twins are coming to visit tomorrow, and all the bedrooms will be full. But please come in and have some milk and cookies."

Jimmy drank the milk and ate the cookies as Mrs. Walters made him a peanut butter and jelly sandwich to put in his bag.

"I hope you find just the right home," she said as he left.

"I will," said Jimmy.

Next he went to Ginger's house. She was his second-best friend next to Steve. Ginger was playing in the yard with her brothers Tom and Marty and her big sister June and the baby Kathleen. Ginger's best friend Phyllis was there too. Jimmy didn't like her very well.

"Hi," he said. "I'm running away and would like to live with you. Can I?"

"I don't know," said Ginger. "I'll ask my mother."

In a little while she came back. "My mother says sorry, but she has enough kids already."

Jimmy wasn't surprised, but he stayed and played awhile anyway. When it was lunchtime, Phyllis went home and Jimmy went into Ginger's house with her. Ginger's mother gave him some potato chips and fruit punch to go with his peanut butter and jelly sandwich.

Jimmy played some more after lunch, but before long he began to wonder where he was going to sleep that night.

"I'd better go," he told Ginger. "I have to find a new home."

"Good-bye," she said. "I hope you find a good one."

The people next door to Ginger were never home, so he didn't stop there. The next house had a big dog that barked and jumped around inside a wire fence. He didn't stop there either.

He crossed the street, looking carefully both ways. Phyllis lived in the house on the corner. She was sitting on the steps playing with her doll, and she stuck out her tongue as he came near.

"Don't bother stopping here," she said. "I'll tell my mother I don't want you."

"I wasn't going to stop anyway," he answered.

Old Mr. MacArthur was down on his knees in the yard, pulling weeds out of the flowers.

"Hello, Mr. MacArthur," Jimmy yelled.

"Oh, hello, young man."

"I'm running away," he said loudly because he knew Mr. MacArthur didn't hear very well.

"Yes, it is a nice day."

"I said, I'm running away," he yelled again.

"There are just too many weeds," the old man muttered. "I can't keep up with them. You come back when you're a little older, Marty, and I'll give you a job."

"I'm Jimmy," Jimmy said.

"Sure you're busy," said Mr. MacArthur. "Everybody's too busy to work any more—even little kids."

Jimmy walked on. He was sure that wasn't the right home.

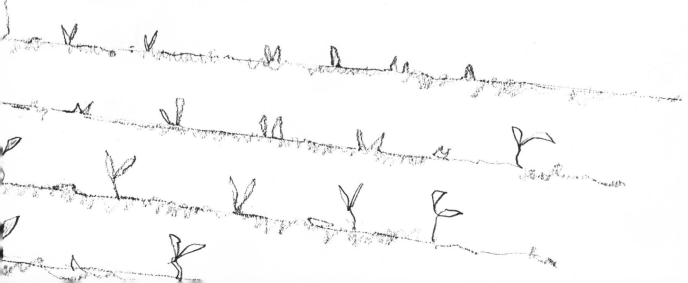

The bag was quite heavy, and he was sorry he had put in the big road grader. The teddy bear and the book and the bubble gum and his clothes would have been enough to carry.

He dug around in the bag and finally found the bubble gum. He chewed it awhile before he went to the next house. The lady was pleasant, but she didn't want a boy either. She already had three cats.

One of the cats was outside, and Jimmy petted and played with it for quite awhile. Jimmy really didn't want to go to the next house. He was afraid they wouldn't want him either. He was afraid his mother was right—running away wasn't as easy as it sounded.

But he did go to the next house, and just as he thought, they didn't need a boy.

By now he was getting hungry again. He knew it must be close to suppertime and soon it would be dark. He was really worried about where he was going to sleep.

He went to three more houses as quickly as he could. Two people were kind and one person was grumpy, but none of them had room for him. The sun was setting, and there was only one house left on the street.

Jimmy stood in front of it a long time, resting the heavy bag on the sidewalk. He was afraid to go to the door. If the people there said they didn't want him, he didn't know where he would go.

Jimmy went slowly up to the house and knocked. A pretty woman opened the door and stood there smiling at him.

"Hello," said Jimmy. "I've been looking all day for a good home. Do you suppose I could live here?"

"Come in," she said. "I've always wanted a little boy just like you."

Jimmy went into the house, feeling a bit shy. He could smell something good cooking on the stove. His stomach gave a little gurgle.

"I really am hungry," he said.

"Wash your face and hands. You're just in time for supper."

When he went out to the kitchen, there was a big plate of spaghetti waiting for him. A man was sitting on the other side of the table.

"Hi," he said. "I hear you're going to be our new boy."

"That's right," said Jimmy happily. He sat down at the table and began to eat.

Running away had turned out all right, after all. He had come to just the right home, the place where he really belonged. Jimmy smiled at his very own mother and his very own father, and they smiled back at him.

J
T

Thompson, Jean

I'm Going to Run Away

	DATE DUE	
JUL 3 0 1978		
NOV 29 '78		
NOV 2 '80		
MAR 2 0 80		
NOV 4 80		
1982		